W9-BSV-980

Julia, Child

words by Kyo Maclear   pictures by Julie Morstad

Tundra Books

To my mother, Mariko (first and best cook).
With thanks to Julie, Tara and Scott
(most marvelous collaborators) – K.M.

To my grandmother, Katie, who always stops
to smell the flowers
(and is an amazing cook) – J.M.

Text copyright © 2014 by Kyo Maclear
Illustrations copyright © 2014 by Julie Morstad

Published in Canada by Tundra Books, a division of Random House of Canada Limited,
One Toronto Street, Suite 300, Toronto, Ontario M5C 2V6

Published in the United States by Tundra Books of Northern New York,
P.O. Box 1030, Plattsburgh, New York 12901

Library of Congress Control Number: 2012950816

All rights reserved. The use of any part of this publication reproduced, transmitted in any form or by any means,
electronic, mechanical, photocopying, recording, or otherwise, or stored in a retrieval system, without the prior written
consent of the publisher — or, in case of photocopying or other reprographic copying, a licence from the Canadian
Copyright Licensing Agency — is an infringement of the copyright law.

LIBRARY AND ARCHIVES CANADA CATALOGUING IN PUBLICATION

Maclear, Kyo, 1970–, author
Julia, child / by Kyo Maclear ; illustrated by Julie Morstad.

Issued in print and electronic formats.
ISBN 978-1-77049-449-7 (bound).   – ISBN 978-1-77049-450-3 (ebook)

I. Morstad, Julie, illustrator II. Title.

PS8625.L435J85 2014   jC813'.6   C2012-906825-X
C2012-906826-8

Edited by Tara Walker

The artwork in this book was rendered in gouache, ink and Photoshop.
The main text was set in Archer Book. The handlettering was rendered by Julie Morstad.

www.tundrabooks.com

Printed and bound in China

1 2 3 4 5 6   19 18 17 16 15 14

To:

_____

You are cordially invited to this tale for all ages about a child named Julia.

While the story contains no true knowledge of (the real) Julia Child and

should be taken with a grain of salt and perhaps even a generous pat of butter,

we hope that you will find something here to savor. If you discover, as we have,

that some stories taste best when shared with others, then all the better.

Bon appétit.

When Julia was very little, she had a splendid meal of sole meunière. And that was that. Julia fell in love with French food. She loved to eat French food. And she especially loved to cook it.

On weekends, she and her friend Simca would shop

at the market and gather new ideas and recipes.

Back home in the kitchen, things didn't always

turn out quite the way they expected . . .

or hoped.

But together they took cooking and baking classes,

and practiced and practiced. And learned a few tricks.

Like many good friends, Julia and Simca sometimes disagreed about little things. But they never disagreed about the larger things.

Sole à la dieppoise
arrange the poached fish
on a ~~tightly~~ heavily
buttered serving platter
and surround them with
the mussels and shrimp
see over

1. Some friends are like sisters.

2. You can never use too much butter.

3. It is best to be a child FOREVER!

When they dreamt of the future, they *always* pictured themselves

cooking happily together: the oldest children in the world.

Life was filled with far too many grown-ups who did not know how to have a marvelous time. The girls had no wish to become big, busy people — wary and worried, hectic and hurried.

One day, Julia and Simca had an idea of how to fix things for themselves and the grown-ups they knew. They would make recipes for growing young.

Each day for a week, they worked on their dishes. They cooked extra slowly to bring out the flavor of not hurrying. They used delicate spices so that worries would disappear and wonders would rise to the surface.

L'ART CULINAIRE

101 DIFFICULT RECIPES

GASTRONOMIE

When they were ready, they set a beautiful table, making sure
the flowers were fresh and all the cups were full.

joie de
vivre
THIS WAY

As the savory scent of cooking wafted through the streets, a curious crowd began to gather. Soon, all sorts of big, busy people wanted a place at the table.

And what a table it was. Fluffy clouds of cheese soufflé. Perfect loaves of crusty

baguette. A golden compote of fresh peaches, sweet as summer sunlight . . .

At first the room was very quiet as the grown-ups nibbled and sampled.

Then the room began to fill with sound. A shriek of pleasure. A shout of delight.

All those big, busy people who were weighed down with worries, who couldn't remember the last time they climbed a tree or even rode a bicycle, who never watched cartoons and only read biographies — well, they began to have a marvelous, rowdy, childlike time.

But then things started to go not so marvelously.

As they ate, the grown-ups began to argue. It seemed they
were very hungry. Too hungry. They were hungry for the fun
they had forgotten and the games they no longer played.
They grabbed the food up all at once, fearful it would not last.

"Just look at them," said Julia. "Where did we go wrong?"

"I think the problem is not that the world is filled

with too many grown-ups," said Simca.

"The problem," said Julia, "is that too many grown-ups

don't have the proper ingredients."

So, for their last recipe, the two friends fixed a few things, adding a
pinch of this and a dash of that. They made smaller portions —
not too little, not too big, just enough to feed the sensible children
from whom these senseless grown-ups grew.

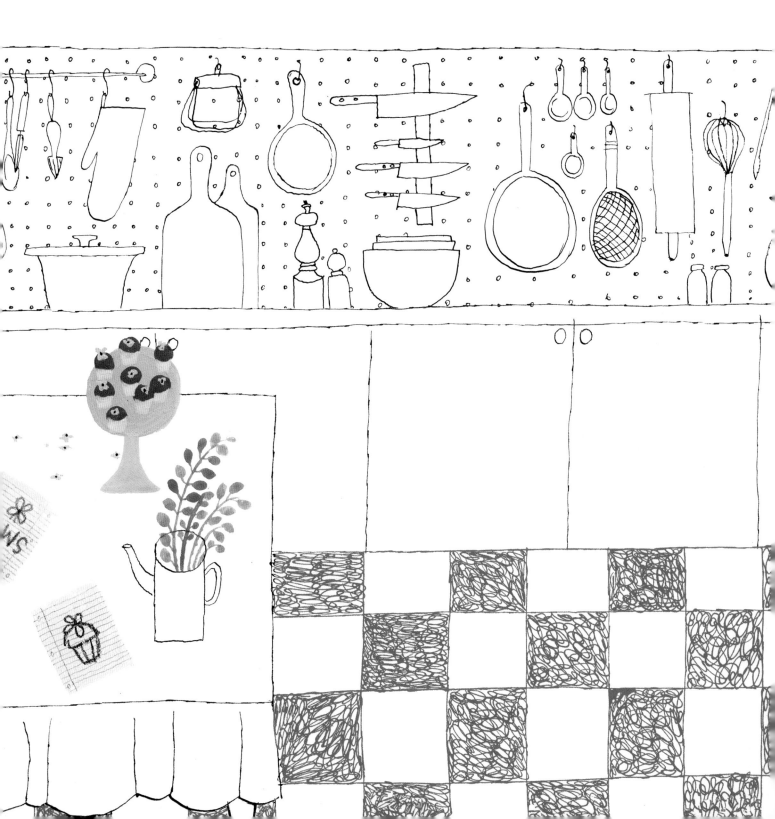

The room fell quiet . . . *petits gâteaux* — chocolate almond cupcakes with chocolate butter icing and the richest, creamiest centers. Each morsel was so delicious.

"There is plenty enough for us all," announced Julia, so the grown-ups would get over their feelings of never-enoughness. And it worked. This time when they ate the cakes, they were a little less beastly and a little more generous.

Well, sort of.

The truth is grown-ups often need some extra help. Baffled and befuddled, mindless and muddled, they sometimes forget what they know.

So Julia and Simca made a cookbook to remind them.